The Divers
and Other Mysteries of Seattle
(and California, but Just a Little)

More Mostly True Stories

Books by Jerome Gold

FICTION
The Moral Life of Soldiers
Sergeant Dickinson (originally titled *The Negligence of Death*)
Prisoners
The Prisoner's Son
The Inquisitor
Of Great Spaces (with Les Galloway)

POETRY
Stillness

NONFICTION
The Divers and Other Mysteries of Seattle
    (and California, but Just a Little)
The Burg and Other Seattle Scenes
Paranoia & Heartbreak: Fifteen Years in a Juvenile Facility
How I Learned That I Could Push the Button
Obscure in the Shade of the Giants: Publishing Lives Volume II
Publishing Lives Volume I: Interviews with Independent
    Book Publishers
Hurricanes (editor)

The Divers
and Other Mysteries of Seattle
(and California, but Just a Little)

More Mostly True Stories

Black Heron Press
Post Office Box 13396
Mill Creek, Washington 98082
www.blackheronpress.com

Cover photograph by Willa Gold.

A shorter version of "Les Galloway" was published by Chronicle Books
as "Les Galloway and the Forty Fathom Bank," the afterword to *The Forty Fathom Bank and Other Stories* by Les Galloway. "All Air is Finite"
and a small part of "The Divers" were originally published in *Prisoners*
by Jerome Gold (Black Heron Press). "I Stepped in Some Shit" was originally published by The Friday's Egg Calendar Company in its 2006 calendar, later in *Moon City Review* and *The New Verse News*. "Runaway"
was also published by The Friday's Egg Calendar Company, in its 2011
calendar.

ISBN 978-1-936364-07-7

Black Heron Press
Post Office Box 13396
Mill Creek, Washington 98082
www.blackheronpress.com

Contents

End of the Rainbow

Driving home on I-5, I pulled off at the rest area at Federal Way for a cup of coffee and maybe a nap. I had finally gotten past the rain and the sky was beginning to open so that it looked like the drive the rest of the way into Seattle would be comparatively easy. I was coming from Corvallis where that morning I had been interviewed about two of my war books. My PTSD had kicked in, though nobody could see it, and I was feeling both tired and hyper alert. Slanting to the right into the exit lane, I noticed a rainbow that appeared to end in the leftmost lane of the interstate about fifty yards ahead of me. I tracked its arc, but lost sight of it behind the evergreens that interceded between the rest area and the freeway.

I did not at first believe I was seeing the end of a rainbow. I would have thought, if ever I thought about rainbows, that they did not end, but simply disappeared; they dissolved into the air, perhaps evaporating with the moisture they lay on. But this one did end. There was no pot of gold, and there were no leprechauns, there was only the leftmost lane of the freeway as you drove north and the rainbow that touched it.

I could not be certain whether or not the pavement was illuminated where the rainbow met it. It seemed to me that it was, but I was aware of the human propensity for self-deception, so I doubted myself. Then I saw a car drive through the rainbow and it appeared to become enveloped in a golden light. Again I doubted what I had seen. Then another car went through it and the same thing happened— the same light. Then a van—the same.

Each vehicle, as it passed through the rainbow, was illuminated for perhaps a second and a half before driving out of the light. I was watching from behind and to the right from where I had stopped at the side of the exit ramp, so I cannot really know how much depth there was to the light, but it took measurable time for each vehicle to drive through it.

I wonder what the occupants of the vehicles experienced. Did they see the rainbow? Were they irritated by the light in their eyes? Did the light seem to them unusual or unusually intense? Did a driver say to the person in the passenger seat, "What the hell was that?"

Now that we know that rainbows have ends, I wonder if this knowledge sheds light, so to speak, on the origins of the myth about rainbows. Certainly it gives credence to the idea of gold, even if not contained in pots, to be found at a rainbow's end.

Liar

Late that afternoon I was driving into the University District from Lake City to pick up my friend Maureen. As I was going up 35th the rain suddenly ended. One moment everything was wet, I had my wipers on, water was running downhill along the curbs, and the next the streets were as dry as the Mojave in summer and I could see shreds of blue through the clouds.

When I got to Maureen's I told her about the rain. She didn't believe me. At her house there was hardly a cloud. "Liar," she said, laughing.

"It's true," I protested. "Just up the hill from the high school, the rain stopped."

"You're lying. You're always lying."

It was true, in a way. I liked making up stories to tell her because I knew she enjoyed hearing them, and she always laughed when she discovered, or I told her, that I had made it up.

"Rain has to stop somewhere," I said. "It doesn't rain everywhere in the world all at once."

She laughed.

"I was in Florida once when the rain stopped in the middle of the street. On one side of the white line it was wet and on the other side it was dry." It was true, but I knew even as I said it that I was defeating myself.

Maureen was delighted. "Liar, liar, pants on fire."

"Is there anything I can do to convince you about the rain?"

"Nope."

She looked at me expectantly, her smile waiting to expand at whatever I said next.

"Well, let's go to dinner. Let's go to that Indian place in Lake City. Maybe it's still raining there."

"It isn't," she said, and laughed.

The Silence of the Tides

We were walking along the sea wall at Alki Beach, Mary
and I. It was the first time we went out, though months
later when we went out again she would not remember our
having dated before.

We would walk for a while, we decided, and then we
would have lunch at Spud's. It was one of those pleasant
days in early summer when it might shower or it might
not, but even if you got wet you would not be overly cold.
We talked quietly, neither of us passionate about what we
were saying. I enjoyed the sound, the texture of her voice.
I noticed that when she used a contraction that had a "d"
embedded in it—didn't, wouldn't—she pronounced the
letter instead of gliding over it or substituting a glottal stop.
(I had taken a linguistics class not long before we met.)

For a moment we were silent. Then, in that silence, I
heard a larger silence. I looked around—the horizon; the
shops and restaurants and beach on the land side—trying
to figure out what it was, and then I looked down into the
water. It was still. There were no wavelets as there had been
a few minutes earlier. It was as if we were standing outside
of time. The tide had been coming in and now it wasn't, but
it wasn't going out either.

And then it was. There was the noise of moving water
again, of Puget Sound withdrawing, of time reversing. I had
never noticed those few minutes in the movement of the tide
when it is at perfect rest, although since that day I have seen
it happen again. But this first time was, I think, the moment
when I began to fall in love with Mary.

Mary

A couple of years after my divorce I began seeing a woman I had met in one of my classes. The class met on Monday, Wednesday and Friday mornings, but I almost always missed the Monday session. I saw my children on weekends and returned them to their mother on Sunday evening and it was hard for me to leave my house on Mondays. My ability to think about anything but the causes of my sadness on that day was nil. Eventually I learned not to take classes that required Monday attendance, but before that I met Mary.

She had noticed my absences and, without asking why, offered to lend me her notes. I thanked her and explained about my weekly depression. Even now, recalling this, I am surprised at how open I was with her without knowing her. She said she knew something was going on with me but hadn't wanted to pry. I thanked her again.

We went to a movie. When I asked her to go, she hesitated but then said she'd like to. I don't remember what the movie was, but there was a scene in it that was filled with violence and I anticipated it and as it began, I put my arm around her and turned her head so that she could hide her face against my shoulder. I asked her if she wanted to leave, but she didn't.

Over coffee, she asked me how I knew that scene was coming up. I didn't know; maybe it was the music or the sudden lack of it. How did I know it would upset her? I didn't know that either; I just thought it would. She thanked me for helping her. That was how she put it: I had "helped" her.

She was small and wiry and she had small breasts. She had dark brown hair and it gave off a rich scent that made me want to protect her from harm. She was matter-of-fact about her body, neither ashamed of it nor liking it much. She said her breasts were beginning to sag. She was twenty-five.

When she was seventeen, she was a fashion model. Once, after a photo shoot, she and some girls she worked with went out to a restaurant. She caught an older man staring at her and she pulled the top of her dress down, exposing her nipples. Telling me, she laughed about the man's reaction, how embarrassed he had been. She compared her breasts now to what they were then.

Once when I went over to pick her up—we were going to see a movie or maybe just out for coffee; there was a wonderful little coffee bar down the street from her apartment building—she said she didn't want to go; her period had started and she needed to stay in. We went into her bedroom and she sat down on a pad she had made of white towels. She didn't use anything to absorb the flow, but bled onto the pad. She was wearing a tee shirt and a loose denim skirt that she had hiked up to her hips to keep it from getting stained. If I was put off, she said, she would understand and we could see each other in a few days, but if I didn't mind it, I could sit with her and we could talk; she would appreciate my company.

She sat with her knees up and I could see the dark hair on her mound and her swollen lips. I could smell the blood as well as the natural scent of her vagina, which I loved. I was aroused, but more than that, the intimacy she allowed me by revealing herself at one of her most vulnerable times prompted in me such tenderness that I could have wept.

As we talked she occasionally checked the towel beneath her. When the blood began to seep through she would get up and put it in a hamper in the bathroom and then return to her bedroom with a fresh towel and sit with me again.

A short time before we started seeing each other, she had ended a five-year relationship with a man she had cared for. He had two children and she missed those kids badly. She missed him too, of course, but she especially missed the children. She talked about her life with them and their father, and said she would have stayed with them forever, but something inside her had changed and she felt she had to leave.

She was only nineteen when she went to live with them. Essentially she had raised those kids, at least until the younger one went into grade school. She didn't regret any of her time with them, but sometimes she thought she was a bad person for having left them. She asked me if I thought she was bad. No, I did not.

Her mother thought she was bad, but that was because of something else. When she was sixteen she began sleeping with a boy she had known all her life. They were always in the same class and hung around together after school. When they began having sex, it was just another thing they did together. She would sometimes spend the night with him. His parents didn't mind that they slept together.

One day her mother asked her where she slept when she spent the night at Mark's house. With Mark, Mary said. At first her mother couldn't believe it, and then she was outraged. And Mark's parents? she asked. Do they know? They don't care, Mary said. A slut, her mother called her. A little whore.

Mary was hurt. She had not seen herself as a whore. What she and Mark did was just… She didn't know. It was a way of enjoying each other. She confided in her friend Juana. Juana was a cheerleader and she turned Mary's mother's accusations into a cheer like you would do at a pep rally.

> A slut, a slut
> All you do is rut
> Spread your legs
> Spread your legs
> Yaaay!

Listening to Juana sing that made Mary feel better, and she and Juana remained best friends. Even today, sometimes Juana would sing it when Mary got blue about herself.

Did I remember that time when I forgot to buy condoms and she said it was all right, don't worry about it? I remembered. Did I think she was on the pill? Yes. I knew you would think that, she said; men always look for an excuse not to use a rubber. Why? Is it so different when you use a rubber? I can't feel as much, I said. I'll use one, but physically it isn't as good.

I'm not on the pill, she said. She didn't use the pill because she didn't like its effect on her body. When I asked what method of contraception she was using, because I had stopped using condoms altogether, she said she was not using anything. She wanted to have a baby. "I'd make one hell of a good mother," she said. That was why she left Robert; she wanted a baby and he didn't want any more.

She waited for me to respond.

I didn't know what to say. Suddenly there was in my

mind a question about how much I could trust her, about how far I was willing to go with her. Until this moment I had not thought about limits; I was in love with her.

I was silent.

She had started seeing a counselor about her feelings at having left Robert and the kids. It had taken her a while to find one who could help her because they tended to feel uncomfortable when she cried. Men did; she didn't want a female counselor. But finally she found a psychologist she liked. She asked me if I would wait for her until after this period of her life had passed, then said before I could respond, "No, you won't. You like women too much."

I may have said, "I'll wait," or I may only have thought to say it, but in either case she turned away from me and I thought then that I had lost her.

Her family lived in Santa Clara and she went there for the holidays at the end of the year. She called me once. During our conversation she said she hadn't slept with anyone since she arrived there. I hadn't thought about her sleeping with anyone but when she said that, I was certain she was either lying or that she intended to go to bed with someone.

When I picked her up from the airport she was distant. She didn't respond to my attempt to hug her and she insisted on carrying her own bags. At her apartment I helped her with her suitcase and then I left.

I didn't call her. She called me twice over the next few weeks but each time the conversation ended without either of us suggesting we get together.

I ran into her seven or eight years later outside University

Book Store in Seattle. She had two daughters now, about four years apart. I tried to talk with them but they were shy and clutched at their mother's skirt. We told each other what we were doing now and she brought me up to date on a couple we had known—separated now, but still friends, she said—and then there was nothing more to talk about. For me there had been a number of women since I had last seen her, and for her there was a man she had met soon after we stopped seeing each other. When I went home I felt again the tenderness I knew when we talked that night as she menstruated onto a white towel, and I mourned the shortness of our lives.

The Power of Love (I)

Saul

I was a gambler. I loved the horses. Not that I made a living
off them. Hell, they made a living off me. Oh, sometimes I'd
win, and sometimes I'd win big. But then I'd play big. Until
the money was gone. Then I'd be back to five- and ten-dollar
bets. Humiliating after I'd won thirty thou, and worse after
I'd lost forty.

Some men were after me. Threatened my wife, my sons.
Told me they would hurt them unless I made good what
I owed. But I couldn't. Where was I going to get twenty
thousand, thirty thousand dollars, I don't even remember
what it was now. So I grabbed Sarah and the kids, took what
we could load in a truck overnight, and left Chicago and
went to L.A.

I was a butcher. Butchering was how I supported my
family and my vice. This was in the days when you still
had butcher shops in your neighborhood, produce stands,
fish markets. This was before the superdupermarkets killed
them all. So I got a job in a butcher shop, gave up the ponies
except for the occasional two-dollar bet, saved my money,
went into partnership with a guy and bought a shop. Sent
the younger son to college, for as long as he wanted to go,
anyway. The older one had some problems and one day the
Sheriff's Department let us know they'd found his body
beside a freeway ramp. OD'd. The people he was with just
dumped him, probably afraid of being found with a body in
the trunk. Broke Sarah's heart.

This was when the horses got back to me. Same story. Won big, played bigger, owed money, they came after me. But this time I fooled them. Before we even got close to them threatening to do bad things to Sarah and my kid, I died. Cancer, big time. And fast. Whoo! Hardly had time to think about it before I was gone.

I'd been up here, or out here, or wherever I am for who knows how long when I ran into my first-born. Still as ding-y as he was down on Earth, or back on Earth, or out there, or wherever it is. Looked a helluva lot healthier though. We didn't have a lot to talk about because we didn't have a lot in common except for Sarah. And that reminded me—I'd forgotten to tell her something. I'd been so involved with dying toward the end, this other thing just slipped my mind.

But how to get in touch with her? I couldn't just go up to her and start talking as if I'd never left. Hell, it'd kill her. Give her a heart attack. I tried talking to her in her sleep, but her snores drove me away. Lying beside her in life, I'd put cigarette filters in my ears, go to sleep that way. But in death I couldn't even pick one up. And I wasn't sure I even had ears—no mirrors up here. Out here. Wherever.

So I had to look for someone else. Found my wife's cousin, but she had her own problems—her husband and his paramour, to use an old-fashioned word—and I didn't want to burden her. Actually, I hadn't known anything about all that until I went looking for Janie and just slipped into her mind. That was how I began to think about it: just slipping into a person's thoughts. Before that thing with Janie, I had never been able to do that. Of course, I had never tried.

What a mess—Janie's mind, I mean. It was everywhere, and going a mile a minute. Well, that's not so fast anymore.

Let's put it this way: it was going a hell of a lot faster than it took me to die, and I went quicker than you could blink. Poor Janie. Well, I had my own troubles and I got out of her head just as soon as I could.

Just for a moment I checked my number two son, but his skull was so thick I didn't think I could get through it to his brain. Speaking figuratively.

I did sneak into one of my sister-in-law's dreams, but, spotting me, she said, "I never liked you." I tried to argue with her, to tell her that her personal likes and dislikes were immaterial now, so to speak, but she ignored me, preferring to concentrate on the exhilaration of a Ferris wheel ride she had enjoyed as a little girl. In fact, she was a little girl in her dream and she was sitting with her father whom I had known, of course, through Sarah. He saw me too, and glared at me, and I figured, "Well, that's that," and took off to look for someone else.

I was trying to remember how long Sarah's father had been dead when I fell into the head of someone I didn't know. That was how it felt, like I'd stumbled and, before I could get my balance, found myself in a young woman's thoughts. And what thoughts! Jeez! I never would have guessed a human being was capable of bringing such things to herself, much less a human being who was only thirty-two years old (how did I know that?) and so pretty and refined-looking (how did I know that? It was dark) that I would have been proud to…to what? I was trying to figure out what she might have meant to me had I been alive too, and at the same time I was crawling out of her mind—that's how it was, as if I was crawling through the jungle of her thoughts and pictures—when she saw me and started shouting, "Wait! Wait! Not yet!" and I felt myself pulled more deeply into this tangle of sensations and images and curse words and this animal need and then there was an explosion of light and then there was nothing at all. In the distance I could hear what I thought was crying, or maybe it was laughter, but I couldn't see anything and anyway the sound was far away and I was exhausted.

I finally found a niece, I think she was, or maybe she was one of Sarah's more distant cousins, who was receptive and didn't want anything in return for doing me this favor. I remember now that she was the one who liked cats. She had four or five from which she'd had the teeth and claws removed. Her husband used to say that the bones were next. Anyway, she was in a trance or something—meditation, I think—when I located her, and I told her I'd left some money in the lining of my favorite sports jacket. I'd sewn it in there because of the people I owed it to: I didn't want them to get it if they found me. Would she please let Sarah know that the money was there? It wasn't much, maybe a couple hundred, but you never knew, she might need it someday.

Well, she did as I asked her to, even letting Sarah know that she'd heard from me. But there was a minor problem: Sarah'd given the jacket to her brother. I'd always liked Lewis because he had such a good heart. A very kind man. And he was the same now—he didn't try to claim the money as his, although he needed it a lot more than Sarah did (how did I know these things?). I tried to get a message to her that, you know, she should give a little of it to him, but in such a way as it didn't look like charity. Actually, for a moment I thought I did kind of influence her, again through her niece, but she put my suggestion out of her mind and kept all the money for herself. She had never liked Lewis' wife who had been a little too…well, let's just say that her heels weren't entirely round, but they were pretty well scuffed. But all that was before she married the baby brother.

Anyway, I wanted you to know all this so you could get some idea of just how persistent is the power of love. It just doesn't let you go, even if you would want it to. That's something I think you should know and think about and maybe act on before it's time to take the dirt nap.

The Power of Love (II)

Lewis

Sarah and I were the youngest. Actually I was the youngest and Sarah was next to me. I had four sisters and no brothers. We were all born in Poland and spent our earliest years there on a farm in a village that is no more. Our father had already gone to America when the war began. This was the First World War.

Unfortunately for us, our village was in a kind of no-man's-land between the Germans and the Russians. First the Germans came and took our cows and horses. Then the Russians came and took our chickens. Then the Germans took our grain. Then the Russians took all the food they could find in our house. Then the Germans took all the food we had hidden. The girls, not only my sisters, but all the girls in the village, shaved their heads to make themselves ugly so they wouldn't be raped. My mother shaved her head too. Both armies did this—stole whatever they could, raped whomever they could, finally left us to starve.

I was very sick when my mother finally decided to leave. I had a fever that would not break and my mother expected me to die at any time. So she and my sisters left me. I don't remember them leaving. I was in a fever and I must have been sleeping or in delirium. I think I remember Sarah crying and kissing me, and my mother slapping her and pulling her away.

I don't know how long it was before I woke. I was sweating but I was very cold. The blanket they had left me was thin, like a filament, like a piece of tissue paper, and I curled up as tightly as I could and returned to sleep.

It was dark when I went back to sleep but it was light when I woke up again. I was very, very hungry, but very, very weak. At first I couldn't walk and I just sat on the side of the bed. I wasn't thinking anything, I just sat there. Then I tried to walk again, and I could, but slowly. I was feeble like an old man, although I was only eleven years old.

I searched the house for food but couldn't find any. If any was left after the Germans and the Russians, my family had taken it with them. I felt weak again and returned to my bed and returned again to sleep.

I was awakened by my bubbi. I was not frightened although I knew she had died when I was five or six. Maybe I was in delirium again, I don't know. Without speaking, she told me to get up and follow her. We went into the kitchen and she pointed to the highest shelf in the cupboard. Then she went away. She disappeared. I did not look for her because I knew she was dead. I found a stool and set it in front of the cupboard and climbed up on it. On the highest shelf, pushed to the back so even a grown man wouldn't have been able to see it, was a loaf of bread so old that mold covered it. I was so hungry that I did not bother to scrape the mold off, but bit into the crust even before I climbed down off the stool. It was hard but I bit through it. I ate some of the bread and then went back to bed. By now, night had come again.

I woke up just before dawn when the sky is gray regardless of how the day will turn out. I was clutching the bread to my chest. I ate some more before getting up from the bed. Then I dressed. I stuffed the bread in my shirt and started out. I did not know where to go, but I walked away from where the sun was coming up.

After several days the bread was gone and I was growing weak again. I tried to beg food from peasants but they had none to give. They were starving themselves. One morning some German soldiers found me as I slept beside the road. After determining that I was not a girl, they directed me to a place where they said I could get food. It was not far, they said. After a half-day's walk, I found it. It was what they called a camp for displaced persons. Now we call such people refugees. I was a refugee.

It was only two or three days before I discovered my mother and my sisters. There were in the part of the camp that housed women and children; I had been put in the men's section. One evening I was sitting with some other orphans, staring over the wire at the women to see what we could, when I saw them: first Rose, my oldest sister, then Esther. They saw me, too. At first we just stared at each other. I could not believe it was them, but also I knew it was them. They waved but I did not wave back. When I saw my mother rushing over to join them, I stood up and turned my back to them and walked into the hut where my bedding was. I did not come out again that day.

But the next day when I went outside they were all standing just on the other side of the wire: my mother, Rose, Minnie, Esther, and Sarah. My mother pointed at me and two soldiers came through a gate I hadn't noticed and came over to me. "Your mother wants you," the one closer to me said. "You're a lucky boy," he said as we walked toward the women's section. His large hand was on my arm above my elbow so I couldn't break loose and run.

That was how I was reunited with my mother and my sisters. Eventually we went to America, but before we could go we were required to suffer even more than we had. Typhus broke out in our camp, and while Minnie and Rose and I and our mother did not catch it, Esther and Sarah did. Esther lost her hair and her teeth, Sarah her hair. Sarah's hair grew back, as did Esther's, but Esther's teeth did not grow back.

Typhus was followed by influenza but somehow we survived it, though all of us got sick. It was 1920 before we left Europe, and good riddance. When I think of what would have happened to us if we had stayed—I do not think of it, and I try not to think of what happened to those who did stay.

In Chicago in America I saw my father again. He was not as large as I had remembered him, but he was still powerful and looked healthy. He was happy to see us. He had made some money and would make more, although he would lose most of it when Prohibition ended.

In Chicago my sisters let their hair grow long and shiny, but my mother continued to cut hers short. She did not trust the Cossacks not to follow her to Chicago. Eventually she would see Death in a dream and she would not leave her bed again except to use the toilet. She died two years after this visitation.

When the Second World War began I was not drafted because I was too old and I had flat feet. Three years later I was not too old and the Army doctor ignored my feet. In the meantime I had married. I was aware of Lillian's reputation, but I did not care. After all, I had made love to many women, and had learned better than to expect an adult woman, especially in wartime, to remain untouched. Also I was very attracted to Lillian and loved sleeping with her.

I was a farrier both before and after the war and worked for the movie studios, keeping the horses shod and healthy, so they could make western movies. When there was not a western in production, I did not work, unless you care to call writing poetry in Yiddish work. Certainly Lillian did not, and during my periods of unemployment life with her was almost unbearable. We have not had a happy time together. Perhaps if my sisters had been more forgiving of Lillian's reputation she would not have turned into the harpy she became.

Sarah was the worst, I think because she loved me most. It was her love for me that I counted on most in my life. So when she asked me to return the checked jacket she had given me, the one that had been Saul's, I did not object. It made me look like a racetrack tout anyway. She had not realized the jacket had such sentimental value for her, she said, until after she gave it away. How could I refuse? It was only when I read Saul's story that I learned there was money in it. Now Sarah is gone too, as are my other sisters, so there is nobody here for me to discuss this with. Soon enough, though, I will see her again, and then we will talk about all that passed between us.

Les Galloway

In 1980, out of money, I took a break from graduate school and went back into the army. I thought I would be stationed in Hawaii but found myself at Fort Baker, on the Sausalito side of San Francisco Bay, and living in the Bachelor Officers Quarters at Presidio. Evenings, I would take a book and walk out to one of the restaurants off post for a cup of coffee. It was important to get away from the army at least once a day if I could.

The first time I saw Les Galloway was in the International House of Pancakes, the IHOP, on Lombard. I was sipping coffee over a book and I heard two people talking about writing. One, a twentyish, black-haired waitress, was saying how much she loved to write, that she wrote every day in her journal and she wrote poetry too. Her writing meant everything to her, she said. She was telling this to an older man dressed in a windbreaker and work pants and seated in a booth at an angle to mine. A manuscript was spread out on the table in front of him.

The man said he did not write poetry. He wrote fiction, although he had written a teleplay on Mark Twain once that had been produced. He started talking craft and authors to her but she withdrew, saying again how much her own writing meant to her. Continuing to eavesdrop, I understood that the man knew what he was talking about and he seemed to have a lot more experience than I had. When the waitress left I thought about going over and introducing myself to him, but I was unable to think of something to say beyond the introduction and so I let the moment pass.

A couple of weeks later I saw him again, this time in the cafeteria at Presidio. In those days the army ran the cafeteria, but Presidio was an open post and the cafeteria was open to civilians. Les was a small man with thin white hair and his right leg was shorter than his left. He used a cane as he walked into the building and he carried a brown paper shopping bag in his other hand. He set the bag down at a vacant table and then got himself a cup of tea and an English muffin and returned to his table with his tray. From his bag he extracted a papaya and a lime. He glanced around the room but did not see me watching him. At least his eyes did not stop at mine. He cut the papaya into halves with a serrated butter knife and then he cut the lime into halves. He scraped the seeds out of the papaya and placed them on a paper napkin on his tray and folded the napkin over them. Then he squeezed lime juice onto the yellow fruit. I would later learn that this was habitually his lunch. Tea or maybe coffee and maybe a muffin, but always a papaya with lime or occasionally a scoop of vanilla ice cream which he would buy at whatever restaurant he was in. He always carried the papaya and the lime in the bag with him, regardless of what restaurant he went into, and in the bag also were manuscripts he was working on and a few books, though all I ever saw him read in a restaurant, other than a manuscript, was the newspaper.

When he was almost finished with the papaya I walked over to his table and introduced myself. I told him I'd seen him talking with the waitress at the IHOP but he didn't remember her or what he had said to her. Still, he was friendly and when I asked if I might sit down with him, he agreed readily.

I told him that I also wrote. When I said this his eyes lost their quizzicality and fixed themselves on me. He mentioned some things about craft and technique and I commented on what he said and he thought about what I had said and commented back. And so we began to trust each other.

He said he had written a novel that he had not been able to place with a publisher. It was titled *The Forty Fathom Bank*. It was too short for a book, editors said, and too long for a story. One journal in the Pacific Northwest had accepted it, then bumped it for a story by Joyce Carol Oates. The editor said if Les could reduce it from one hundred pages to six the magazine would publish it. Les refused and decided that he could not stand Joyce Carol Oates' writing.

He did not like Henry Miller either, did not like him personally. Once, in the Fifties, Les was in a jazz bar when Henry Miller and his wife came in. There were a couple of empty chairs at Les' table and Miller asked if they could sit there. After the set, they talked about this and that and then about writing and Les said something witty, catching Miller by surprise. Miller turned to his wife and said, "Isn't it amazing what you can find in some of these places?" Les never forgave him that, that arrogance that placed him at a station below Miller's own, and he had not read any of Miller's work since.

He did like Dreiser's work and he liked Djuna Barnes' *Nightwood* and said she had really known Paris whereas Hemingway had not, though how he could know who had known what, he did not say. He liked Jean Rhys' writing. I had not read her and he said he would lend me a couple of her books. We agreed to meet the next Saturday and exchange manuscripts.

We met again at the Presidio cafeteria. I handed over a manuscript copy of my novel, *The Negligence of Death*, and he gave me a copy of *The Forty Fathom Bank* and a book by Jean Rhys, *Good Morning, Midnight*. He settled in to eating his papaya while I read the first paragraphs of his manuscript. I could see it was something I would want to pay attention to and I set it aside, telling Les I would read it later in my room. He had been watching me as he ate and after I said this he relaxed and said he would read my book later too, when he was alone.

We talked writing again. He had had a story published in *Esquire* back in the Forties, and another one in *Prairie Schooner*. He was not enthusiastic about academic publications, because nobody read them, he said, but he was pleased that *Prairie Schooner* had done "Where No Flowers Bloom." We sat for a while without speaking.

It was an exceptionally clear day, I remember, and as we looked out at the bay through the big windows Les remarked how close the land on the other side appeared on a sunny day when there was no mist. He used to teach fiction writing at Fort Mason, he said, and he once had a student, an elderly woman, who had been a little girl at the time of the San Francisco earthquake and fire. Her mother had taken her out on a ferry with other people fleeing the fire and the ferry had brought them all out to the middle of the bay where it was safe and had stopped so they could see the city burn. She told the class seventy years later how it had looked, the city burning down to the water, how she had seen the section where her house had been all red with the fire's glow, how worried she had been about her father and her brother who had stayed behind. She had held the class in thrall when she told this, but she did not write a word about it. Instead, she wrote light romances.

Les and I got together again the following week. Each of us had wonderful things to say about the other's work. His little book seemed to me a near-perfect piece of writing. The character development was solid, and the book had a theme! I was not accustomed to recent American novels, other than some science fiction, having something to say about the nature of our species. I told Les this. He came back with "Character and theme are everything. If you have character and theme, everything else will follow." He wagged his finger at me as though he were a schoolmaster trying to impress his student to remember something.

For his part, he liked *Negligence of Death*, saying it reminded him of Camus' *The Stranger*. I had not thought of that. I knew that I had been heavily influenced by Camus but I did not recall having thought of him as I was writing *Negligence*, at least not consciously.

I asked Les about Conrad. It seemed to me that *The Forty Fathom Bank* was a kind of converse of *The Secret Sharer*. Les said he had read *Heart of Darkness* while writing his book and thought that might have been an influence. I mentioned *The Secret Sharer* again but Les only shrugged. I think now that I was right, that Les had modeled *The Forty Fathom Bank* on *The Secret Sharer* but had not wanted to admit this to me.

In 1982 I left the army and returned to Seattle to finish graduate school. In the fall I went to Samoa to do anthropological fieldwork. While there I met an American who, though earning his living as a teacher in Samoa, was also an editor for a small press in Milwaukee. It had published one book and on its title page was "Milwaukee and Pago Pago," which meant that while John lived in (or near) Pago Pago, the other editor lived in Milwaukee. The book they had published had been written by the Milwaukee editor. John said they were looking for other manuscripts. I wrote Les, asking him to send me *The Forty Fathom Bank*. I gave it to John as soon as I received it. He liked it very much and sent it to his co-editor. They had an arrangement whereby both had to agree to publish a book; neither had the authority to acquire a book on his own.

The Milwaukee editor turned it down. The rejection letter was perfunctory, but he told John that if Les were a younger man he would be willing to publish the book, but since Les was not young—

John was dumbfounded and I was angry. To both of us a book was to be judged by its quality, regardless of who wrote it. I suspected that John's co-editor had been threatened by Les' manuscript, that he was afraid it was better than his own book. Years later, John told me that he eventually reached the same conclusion. The press finally died because John's friend would not agree to publishing another book.

But I had learned some of the rudiments of publishing from listening to John. He had been an editor for the University of California at Berkeley and was a poet and literary critic himself. So he knew publishing, at least certain aspects of it, from both the publisher's vantage point and the author's.

When I returned to the United States I went to San Francisco to see Les. I suggested we publish his book ourselves. Les equivocated. He did not like the idea of being both author and publisher. My argument was this: Editors select books for publication that fall within the parameters set by the companies they work for. Les and I both knew he had written a good book. Quality was not the issue. The issue was the acquisition policies of the large publishing houses. Still, Les was unsure. Finally I said: "How will you feel five years from now if you don't do it?" And so we put together our own press, Black Heron Press, to publish *The Forty Fathom Bank*.

His early life had been one of adventure. He had sailed to the South Pacific on the last clipper ship to put out of San Francisco. He had fallen in love with a prostitute in New Zealand and jumped ship in Hawaii, having fallen in love with another woman. Later he was a motorcycle courier for a Bolivian general during a war against Paraguay. Always an admirer of competence, he deserted because he did not think the general knew what he was doing. Following his travels in South America, Les lived in Mexico City for a year. Except for one unpublished novel, *Beyond the Dark Mountain*, much of which concerns a Pacific voyage, he did not write about any of this. Instead, he wrote some exquisite stories about the sea, including *The Forty Fathom Bank*, "Where No Flowers Bloom," and "The Albacore Fisherman."

When he was sixty he began work on *Beyond the Dark Mountain*, finishing it almost ten years later. He met with the usual responses when he sent it out: editors did not read it but pretended they had and sent it back, or they did not send it back. Mostly they ignored it. Finally an editor from a local publishing house did read it and liked it and offered Les a contract. The week before they were to begin editing, the entire fiction staff, including Les' editor, was fired. The publisher had decided to cease publishing fiction. Three or four years later, Les told me that he had been disappointed and angry, but he had also felt relieved. Publishing that book, he believed, would have changed his life and he did not want it to change. He continued sending the manuscript around but nothing happened and I think he regarded sending it out as a matter of duty rather than desire. We never talked about publishing it through Black Heron Press, if for no other reason than that it was very long and we could not have afforded it.

Beyond the Dark Mountain is fictionalized autobiography. Its first chapters are taken directly from Les' childhood. As a boy, Les developed a high fever and had to be hospitalized. Hospital care was costly, his father, an itinerant preacher, was away on one of his jaunts, or perhaps he had left for good by that time, and Les' life was at risk. His mother, an attractive, sensual woman, slept with the attending doctor in order to ensure Les' care.

This is an old story, of course, a mother's sacrificing her honor for her child, but it is no less poignant for the retelling. When, after I read those passages, Les told me explicitly what had only been implied in them, he alternately spoke and puffed at the pipe he was trying to light, but all the while he watched my eyes. For my part, I tried to reveal nothing, to convey only that I accepted what he said as one accepts life. He said he never learned the nature of the fever he had had, but it left him with a stiffened hip and a leg that would not grow much longer.

I never knew a man who so enjoyed the company of women. It has been said so often that most men do not like women that it sounds true even if it is a suspect truth. Still, I never met a man who liked women more than Les did. His skin took on a blush and his eyes glistened when he was with a woman he was attracted to. But if women were his joy they were also his sadness, for he was haunted by them.

I believe he felt indebted to them as he felt indebted to his mother. He married several times, each wife but one flawed in the same way as the others, fathered several children and raised all but one himself. He and I never talked about friendship or love, though we discussed love's delusions and, of course, its betrayal. When the sexual urge finally left him, he told me it was a relief, he did not miss it a bit.

Until he became too ill to write, he worked on another novel, a kind of love story. (One must always qualify the genre with Les: *The Forty Fathom Bank* is a kind of sea story but also it is a tale of greed and the failure of redemption.) I never saw it and, as far as I know, no copy exists. Convinced by a friend that the story was not up to the standard Les set with *The Forty Fathom Bank* and the best of his stories, he destroyed it. Here is its plot as I remember his telling it to me.

A young man travels to Utah from California. In Salt Lake City he falls in love with a girl. However, requiring specialized surgery, he must go on to New York. He is in love but also he is looking forward to meeting some of New York's fabled elegant women. In New York he undergoes surgery and stays on to recuperate. He and his love correspond but then she stops writing. He has not been faithful and wonders what she might know, what she might have gleaned from the subconscious aspect of his letters. Finally, out of guilt and remorse, he writes her a vicious letter, ending their relationship.

Decades later, an elderly man, he returns to Salt Lake

City. He searches out the family of the girl he loved and from them he learns that she died in an automobile accident while he was in New York. From the dates on her headstone he understands that she was already dead when he wrote the vile letter.

This story is so essentially Les: the flaw of character, the minor decision that takes on tragic significance, the base act that exposes the actor to himself, the ghostly echoes that arise from that act.

I knew him for only the last ten years of his life. He wrote well until a year or two before he died, when physical pain and medication confounded that special clarity of mind he needed to write. His last decade, it seems to me, was an itemized giving-up of everything that was important to him, including any attempt to resolve the conflicts that had beset him early on. His writing showed no resolution. (Were he able to read these last sentences, his eyes would flash and he would turn away in contempt. "Writing is not about resolution," he would say. "It is about conflict and conflict is never resolved.") It showed, instead, wonderment and knowledge. He believed in Nothing as though it were Something. Yet despair was foreign to him. Writing for a few friends, he told me, was enough for him. Had anyone else said this, I would not have believed him. But Les was so lacking in self-pity that I took him at his word. He did that, writing for his friends, as long as he was able.

The phone rang at half past midnight and I thought immediately of Les. Who else would call at this hour? I did not want to get out of bed and I let the machine take the call. I listened for a voice and when it didn't come I was even more certain that it was he, for he hated talking to my machine. I promised myself that I would call him back but I did not call. I had talked with him a week or two earlier and he had sounded so depressed—he was weak from the dialysis, he said—that I was reluctant to talk with him again so soon. He had asked when I would be coming down to San Francisco. I told him I did not think it would be before August or September and he said he did not think he would be alive then. I had never heard him sound so tired. I did not try to joke with him. We talked a little about books and then we hung up.

On Thursday, May third, 1990, a message from his daughter Lisa was on my machine when I came home from work. Les had died—"passed away"—the Sunday before. It was a stroke. He had expected to die from an aortic aneurysm he had been cultivating. Instead, it was a blood clot that had traveled to his brain from his foot.

A final vignette. This was told to me by a friend of Les. In the late Eighties when *The Forty Fathom Bank* had been out for several years, he and Les had gone to dinner at a very good fish place in San Anselmo. It was a weekend evening and the restaurant was packed, the tables pushed so closely together that you could not help but hear your neighbors' conversation. At the table nearest Les and Tom was a couple engrossed in talk about fishing and books. They were very young, in their earliest twenties, but they knew what they were talking about. Les figured the young man must be a commercial fisherman and both he and his woman friend knew the best books about the sea. Before either of them could object, Les had joined in their conversation and in a moment the young man turned to him and said, "Oh, next you'll be telling us you're the author of *The Forty Fathom Bank!*"

Les, of course, was both surprised that they knew the book and delighted that they did. He introduced himself, putting the surprise back on them, and in a moment the conversation included both tables.

Gravity

Sylvia Browne, the famous psychic, best-selling author, and founder of her own church, tells us that the Other Side is not a religious or ideological concept, but is an actual place located three feet above what we know as Earth. It is distinct from our Earth insofar as it exists in a dimension apart from those we recognize.

Actually, I suspected as much. Not the part about the Other Side being in another dimension, but that it is a place contiguous with our own world. I have thought this was true ever since I was nine years old and something or someone smacked me on the butt when I had it elevated as I hunkered down on my elbows in my bedroom, reading a comic book. As I recall, the smack didn't hurt; it was, rather, as if someone had been walking by and decided in passing to swat me on the butt.

In a trice I was on my feet, searching the corners of my room for the perpetrator. I had, after all, thought I was alone, and the door was closed, as I had left it. Finding no one, I sought out first my mother, then my father, and finally my sister, asking each in turn if she or he had just been in my room. In turn, each said no. I believed them, as they all looked at me as if I were genuinely nuts. Why was I asking? my mother wanted to know. She was hanging clothes on a line in the backyard and she had a clothespin in her mouth, but I understood her.

"Someone just hit me on the butt," I said.

My mother laughed but she kept the clothespin in her mouth and her laughter came around it on either side, making little puffing sounds. "Go ask your father," she croaked.

I found my father lying on his side on the front lawn, a pile of crab grass near his left arm, a trench knife in his right hand, digging in the dirt in front of him. He also asked why I was asking.

"Someone just hit me on the butt."

"You probably deserved it. When are you going to come out here and help me weed the lawn?"

I pretended I hadn't heard him and went back inside the house and into my sister's room where she was playing house and talking with her invisible friend and I accused her of going in my room when I wasn't looking and hitting me on the butt.

She laughed, but then she started to cry and said she was going to tell our mom that I was accusing her of things. As I left her room, I heard her cry change to a laugh again.

This was the first incident I can recall for which there was no explanation other than the one I came up with, to wit: someone from another, invisible, dimension had crossed into our world, smacked me on my butt, and ducked back into his or her own world.

As I grew older, I found myself bumping into things that were not there, and I often thought that the same person who swatted me on the butt was placing invisible coffee tables, chairs, kitchen counters in my path, then whisking them away as soon as I had walked into them. These encounters were, on occasion, painful and always discomforting, but when I looked for such evidence as I could show my parents, like a bruise, I found nothing at all. Evidence was important because my regular complaints about invisible beings from another dimension victimizing me just about had my parents convinced that I was well and truly crazy, and they were talking about sending me to a military boarding school.

As I grew older I grew taller, and the things I bumped into, at least the invisible ones, grew higher. It seems to me now that whatever it was I connected with, it was always at hip or thigh level. Nowadays, though I no longer bump into invisible things, my hip is about three feet off the ground, where Sylvia Browne tells us the Other Side exists. I wonder, though, if she is wrong, if the Other Side resides at, say, two feet above the earth, for this would have been the altitude of my hip when I was eleven or twelve and sorely encountering invisible objects most frequently.

Another thing that bothers me about this three-foot dictum is the matter of gravity. If Sylvia Browne is right about the location of the Other Side, or even if she's wrong and it's two feet off the ground rather than three, this means the world the dead live on is larger than our world. Here is the math. The diameter of the earth is approximately 7,957.7285 miles. As there are 5,280 feet per mile, we multiply 7,957.7285 by 5,280 and get 42,016,806 feet. But given that the Other Side is four to six feet wider than our earth, albeit in the same location as our world, its diameter is between 42,016,810 and 42,016,812 feet. Another way of conceptualizing this is to look at the diameter of the Other Side as between 7,957.7285 miles plus four feet and 7,957.7285 miles plus six feet.

This is worrisome. As everyone knows, the earth spins on its axis at a certain rate of speed. The exact rate is not important for our discussion. What is important is that the speed of spin is gradually slowing, such that in several billion years objects on the surface of the earth will begin to fly off into space. Remembering our high school physics, we recall that objects farthest from the center of gravity— in this case, somewhere around the center of the earth—are least affected by gravity. In other words, when the world loses spin enough, the dead who live on the Other Side will be flung into space even before we the living are. They will die first. This is worrisome, as I say, because when we pass over, our loved ones who have preceded us will already have passed on again. But where? Is there another aspect to the Other Side, one that we don't yet comprehend? Is there another Other Side?

Oh, Those Prankster Angels

Some people say you should always trust your spirit guides from the Other Side, that they have your interests at heart. I say no. They may, but they may not. They are tricksters. They lie. You can't trust them. Look at what happened to a publisher I know and an author he admired.

Susan wrote a book—a wonderful book, both a love story and a spiritual quest written to capture the hearts and yearnings of as many people as possible—and eventually found a publisher. I say "eventually" because finding a publisher, even for a book as wonderful as Susan's, is no easy thing. But enough about that. The point is that she did find a publisher.

He did not have a lot of money, but he hoped that Susan's book would make it for him. He published only a few books a year and had never had a hit. Oh, occasionally he garnered a minor profit from a book, but he'd never published one that was a smash-down, balls-to-the-wall, go-for-the-moon financial success. But enough about old dreams.

While the book was being edited, Susan and her publisher had many conversations about it and about the assurances she was getting from her guides, who were not yet known— to Susan and her publisher, at least—to be pranksters. Her guides, Susan said, were telling her her book was going to be a roaring success. In fact, the marketing person for Susan's book was herself convinced that, with the right nudging, the book indeed could make some money. (The marketing person also believed in guidance from the Other Side and, unknown to Susan and her publisher, believed, too, that everything written in the *National Enquirer* was true.) Susan made plans to give up her job in real estate.

The publisher, a man of some experience in the publishing world, was less sanguine. His experience with authors who said they would do *anything* to promote their book was that, once the book was in print, they usually wouldn't. Oh, they believed it when they said it, but then there were a thousand reasons not to do this or that. Some even denied having made that commitment. Still, the publisher could not help being swayed by Susan's enthusiasm, and sometimes he actually found himself asking her, "What do your people on the Other Side say?" Susan consistently reported that her guides were as enthusiastic as she herself was. The publisher decided to increase the print run by a factor of three. Susan gave notice.

The book came out just as the United States invaded Iraq. Public attention was on things Arabic, on things Middle Eastern, on things military and presidential. Two wholesalers who specialized in spiritual books gave up the ghost, so to speak. At the same time, the two most influential magazines that reviewed books concerned with matters of the spirit also went under. The marketing person reported that the producers of radio shows that had always been interested in metaphysics and paranormal phenomena were not returning her calls.

The book sold two hundred copies.

Susan was out of work.

Her publisher, ridden with debt, stopped publishing and began looking for a job.

The marketing person was out of work.

Sometimes, at four in the morning, the publisher woke

up, alert to the merest nuance of sound and shadow, and wondered whether or not his life had meaning. At other times, falling into and out of sleep after going to bed, he was certain he heard Susan's guides laughing maliciously.

He called Susan and left her a message asking what she thought of her guides. She delayed responding, but finally did, informing him that her guides had assured her that all had happened as it was meant to. All she could think, she said, was that her book was meant to fall into the hands of someone it would benefit, although her guides had not told her this. Not precisely. Not, in fact, in any way. Sometimes, she said, the Other Side worked this way. It did something ostensibly to affect one person, but really to benefit someone else.

But she was happy that her book had been published and, incidentally, she did not accept that it had sold only two hundred copies, and her attorney would be contacting the publisher next week. In the meantime, he would be happy to know that she had found another job, one she thought her talents were more suited to, as an insurance agent. So things had worked out, although not in the way she had anticipated.

Nor in the way the publisher had anticipated. He had no doubt Susan's book had benefited someone—books do that, after all; in this, he had faith—but was the benefit to this unknown reader worth the disaster to him, the publisher? If someone's life was at risk, couldn't the Other Side have saved it in a way that was less catastrophic to him and to all those authors he would not be publishing, no longer having a publishing company to do this?

Ultimately he decided that Susan's guides had indeed

achieved what they intended. But what they intended was to entertain themselves by destroying his life. He heard them laughing every night now, preventing him from sleeping. The only way he found to silence them was to concentrate on how he would word his résumé.

Runaway

for Leah

I left Seattle because my friends were dying.
Nathan O.D.'d.
Rebel drove into a wall.
Pale Mary suicided down
in California.
Krystal got killed in front of the Jack in the Box.
That was where Lindsey was shot the year before.
Mia—everybody knows about Mia.

Nathan O.D.'d. We were sitting around.
We watched him shoot. He knew he was doing
too much. We knew, too. But none of us
said anything, and Nathan...he knew what he
was doing. He was smiling, and then he
fell over. The needle was still in his arm.
That was it, really. That was what told me to
get out of Seattle.

What happened to Mia, too. Everybody knows
what happened to Mia.

My mother thinks I ran because somebody
molested me, or worse. Maybe
somebody in the family. Maybe my uncle or my cousin.
That never happened.
I ran because my friends were dying.

Portland's O.K.

I Stepped in Some Shit

for G.W. Bush

I stepped in some shit. It was round, not like
a cow's or a buffalo's, but like a
bear's, or a human being's. It wasn't
like a dog's. It was too thick, too perfectly
round, round without seam. It had too much heft
to be a dog's. Or so it appeared.

It could have been a human's, or a bear's.
It was about a foot long and, as I say,
almost perfectly round. There were no
wrinkles, no indentations. There were
no imperfections, none to be seen on the
surface, at least. The coloring was
uniform, a rich brown.

I was out walking. Taking a stroll
following my afternoon coffee.
It was a nearly glorious day: sun,
large, white clouds to make you think sailing
ships and the sea, a breeze with the
occasional gust to say, six knots.
Light-jacket weather; a thin windbreaker.
And there it was, on the sidewalk. (It was
probably not a bear's.) I saw it.
I stepped in it.

The Divers

Harry went into the water a mile east of Alki Beach. Twenty years earlier there had been an abandoned cannery here, its windows broken, the green paint on it sides worn past flaking and slowly disappearing under pressure of rain and sun. Divers called it the ugliest building in Seattle and used it as a point of reference, as in: "Go out toward Alki. Look for the ugliest building in Seattle. I'll meet you just to the left of it and we'll go in there."

Now, instead of the cannery, there was a park. Grass, sun shelter, rest rooms. Visually an improvement, but it brought people. Harry did not like to be around people he did not know well. He would look at them and guess what they were capable of, but he didn't know what they would do, or when. He was a rehabilitation counselor in a prison for children.

Today he was diving without a partner. When he dived alone he preferred to go to a place he knew, where he was familiar with the currents and was not likely to run into discarded fishing line. Fifteen years ago, maybe more, he had gotten tangled in line near the Fauntleroy ferry dock while swimming through a kelp bed and had to rely on his partner to cut him out of it. He had been snagged before he knew it. Still, if there were no fish to attract fishermen, there was little to attract him. Fauntleroy was not a place he would dive alone now. In any event, there was only a vestige of the kelp bed that had been there. Most of it had been torn away by a gale a few years back.

The day had started out clear but by the time he got in the

water a thin layer of cloud concealed not only the sun but the entire sky, so that what he could see beneath the surface was negligible. There was a small school of striped perch and he had a glimpse of a dogfish in the murk at the edge of visibility. He was out of the water after thirty minutes, though he had air enough for another fifteen.

He went out again a few days later, this time to the pilings at Edmonds. He was with Bruce. The pilings were what remained after Chevron took out the oil pipeline and dismantled the dock where the tankers used to put in. Though it was the beginning of winter, there had been several warm, sunny days and the algae bloom was so thick they could hardly see their hands until they got down to thirty feet. At the bottom they saw a large cabezon, some tube worms attached to the pilings, and a sponge that Bruce picked up and used in the pretense of washing his armpits. He often played the clown and his silliness as often made Harry laugh.

When they came out of the water Harry found that the fin strap behind his left ankle had been cut through so that only a narrow strip of rubber held it together. When he looked closely he saw serrations, like tooth marks, at the edges of the cut. He remembered then that as he had settled himself on his belly to observe the cabezon, he had pushed his foot back and something had hit him. He had thought a piece of trash had fallen on him, maybe a bit of rotting timber. It didn't hurt so he didn't think more of it, but now he thought it must have been a wolf eel. He had seen one here before, in ten feet of water, eating a rock crab.

The next week they went to the same place. It had gotten cold again and Bruce wanted to see what he could see with good visibility. Harry had a bad feeling even before they went in the water and he was tired in a way he couldn't explain. His sense that something was wrong intensified and halfway to the end of the pilings, while they were still on the surface, he told Bruce he wanted to turn back.

There was a lot of chop accompanied by tidal swells and they decided to submerge and swim back to the beach under water. When Harry took his first breath his regulator went into free-flow. He couldn't stop it; air was gushing through his mouthpiece too fast to breathe it in. He went to the surface, Bruce following, and inflated his buoyancy compensator and asked Bruce to turn off his air. They snorkeled back to the beach.

Harry had his tank refilled at the dive shop beside the small marina a quarter mile from the pilings and rented a regulator there. They had decided to do a night dive in the underwater park north of the ferry terminal. They were into winter now and they had only an hour to wait until the gray northern light was gone. They sat over coffee at the Skipper's near the terminal.

Bruce had recently separated from a woman he had lived with for four years. Harry had always enjoyed diving with him and Bruce was eager to get into it again. Janice had convinced him to give it up, he said, after they started talking about getting married. It wasn't the risk, he thought, because he had taken up mountaineering after he stopped diving and she hadn't said anything about that.

Harry knew Janice and it did not make sense to him that she had insisted Bruce quit diving; the three of them used to dive together. But it was true she hadn't gone out in a while when he gave it up. Maybe there had been an agreement: he gives up something, she gives up something. Each sacrifices something for the marriage. Harry had known other couples to do this. In any case, he liked Bruce and was glad to be diving with him again.

Setting his cup down, Bruce said he thought he and Janice had made a mistake by getting engaged when they were just fine living together. He hoped they would remain close, or become close again after her anger had lost some of its bite.

"She's hurt," Harry said.

"Well, yeah." Bruce laughed ruefully. "She's kind of unpleasant to be around right now."

"Are you still seeing each other?"

"We're trying to. It's not like it was, but maybe it will be."

Harry didn't say anything.

"She'll never forgive me." He gave that laugh again.

Harry didn't say anything.

"I wish I hadn't asked her to marry me. I wish I hadn't broken off the engagement." A grim smile. No laugh.

"Do you still want to marry her?"

"I never did. I mean if I wanted to get married, I'd want to marry her. But I don't want to get married. Not now, anyway. Maybe not ever. I'll be like you."

"I was married once."

"Yeah? I never knew that." Bruce looked at him. "What else don't I know about you? Are you keeping secrets?"

Harry laughed.

"How's the work?" Bruce asked.

Harry shrugged. He said, "We had a suicide. Not my

unit, one of the girls' cottages. Hanged herself in the shower. I didn't know her, fortunately."

"Jesus," Bruce said. "What do you do in a situation like that?"

"I wasn't there. I was in my own cottage when it happened. We locked down. All the cottages locked down while Security dealt with it. Oh, you mean personally?" Harry thought for a moment. "I don't know. I don't know what I do. I try to help the kids deal with it. There are always some who feel responsible even if they didn't know her. As if there was something they could have done to prevent it."

"There've been others?"

"This is the third since I started there. There have been dozens of attempts. It's a pretty unhappy place."

"I don't know how you do it."

Harry pushed back from the table. "Ready to get wet?"

"I owe you an explanation," Harry said. They were in the car. "About why I wanted to turn back."

"At the pilings? You had a premonition, didn't you?"

"How did you know that?"

"It was pretty obvious. You said you wanted to abort and then your regulator fell apart. It doesn't take a genius to put that together. Plus, you've had them before, haven't you? Didn't you used to get them when you were parachuting?"

"Once, yeah. I forgot I told you about that."

"And you were right again. I trust you, old man. We've always had that agreement, remember? If one of us doesn't feel good about it, we abort the dive. Right?"

"Right."

"Okay then. How do you feel about this one?"

"It's going to be something to behold."

"My feeling exactly."

They were in the parking lot and Harry pulled into a space. Two other cars were in the lot but no one was on the beach except for an elderly woman walking a terrier. They changed into their wet suits in the rest room at the far end of the park. It was cold and their suits were still wet from the afternoon. Both of them were shivering. By the time Harry got his tank on he wanted only to get in the water and get moving.

The visibility was good and they submerged about twenty minutes from the beach. He could see Bruce eight or ten feet ahead, swimming toward the wreck. There were two wrecks actually, and they passed the remains of the first, about the size of a dory, and went for the one nearer the ferry dock. They were sailing along the bottom—that was how it felt, as though he were sailing with the wind behind him, so effortless was the swim in the cold, almost still water—and found the boat at forty feet. Bruce gestured and they went up over the top of it and started down toward its deck.

To Harry's right, out of the gloom, a small lingcod swam into the beam of his lamp, turned and swam back into the dark. As he approached the deck, the fish came again, mouth agape, teeth screening the pit, and again was gone. It was young, twelve or fifteen pounds. Harry pressed air into his b.c. and hung in the water, motionless, waiting for it to come a third time. When it did, he saw a gray film where its right eye should have been, and that it always swam away to its left, following its good eye.

He trailed his light after it, saw its shadow run along the

ruined boat deck, saw it turn again toward the light, now fully in the beam, now gone. Bruce was resting on his knees on the deck. As the fish passed, its blind eye to him, he put his hand out, then pulled it back before the fish ran into it.

How had it happened? Had it been hooked, then the hook torn out? Had it been attacked? What would have attacked it? Whatever happened, it must have happened here. It could not have found its way here half-blind. It would never find its way anywhere else now. Circle after circle, it would swim until it was no longer able. What was it Harry saw in its good eye? Madness? Rage? Did it know it followed only itself? Be careful, Harry told himself. What are you giving it and what is there without you? He hung in the water, his lamp in his hand. The fish followed itself into light, into darkness, into light...

Harry checked his air. He had seven hundred pounds left. How long had he been hanging here? He kicked down to where Bruce was and showed him an open hand and two fingers from the other one. Bruce checked his gauge, then showed it to him. He had a little less than Harry. Bruce jabbed his thumb toward the surface and they ascended.

Harry took his regulator out of his mouth. "Wow."

"Right." Bruce looked around as though to get his bearings. "Look." Perched on a resting raft less than five meters away, a cormorant was staring at them. It took off, almost belly flopping into the water before it caught air. It was about the size of a herring gull and a half again.

As they were changing into their clothes, Harry said, "I wish we could have killed it. It's going to starve."

"It's a state park. You can't do anything about what you see. If the rangers catch you, they'll fine the shit out of you."

"You can't do anything about what you see."

"That's what I said."

"I know."

"In a way, that's what I like most about diving. You're the alien. It's like you're a guest on another planet and one of the rules is you can look, but you can't touch, at least not in a protected area."

"Even if you see suffering."

"Yeah. Even then. It's rough."

"Well, you're right when you say it's like being on another planet. For me, it's like stepping into a science fiction novel, and the beings in it don't give a damn about you as long as you don't try to eat them. It's their world and you're going to be there for only a few minutes. The problem comes when we care about them. We want to put an end to their suffering, or what we imagine is their suffering, even if we have to kill them to do it."

"Whoa, Harry. You've been reading too much. I just do it for fun."

"Oh no, my furry friend. I know you. You're lying to yourself."

"I know, but it's a good lie." Bruce giggled like a ten-year-old. "My furry friend," he said, looking at Harry. He repeated the child's laugh.

Harry had used to dive with a man who had retired from teaching. Harry asked him once if he missed it. Every day, he said. He missed the kids. He missed watching them develop into something more than they had been, or at least something different. But he did not miss the administration.

He did not miss its insistence on teachers giving up something that worked for something that didn't. He did not miss taking orders from people who had no experience of the classroom, or who ignored what they had learned when they were teachers. He did not miss the ideologues, the religionists, or the false patriots. Eventually he realized that his daily experience with kids no longer compensated for everything about the administration that so weighed on him. He felt his life no longer had balance and he decided to retire. He became a fine printer, using an old Chandler and Price letterpress to produce chapbooks and the occasional perfect-bound book.

Harry thought about what Mark had said, especially the part about compensation and balance, and thought too about what he might do if he gave up the prison. His father had left him some money and he thought he could live off it for a couple of years if he had to. He wrote a letter of resignation, leaving space for date and signature, folded it into a small rectangle and put it in his wallet.

They were Dungeness. Harry was at seventy feet when he saw them, Bruce on his right and a little above. The crab were moving in a column of twos toward the beach, coming up from where it was too dark to see them and too deep to dive. Every few meters Harry saw one or two out at either side of the column, like flank scouts. Two crab in the column, marching side by side, grasped something thin and white like a piece of a tee shirt between them, the left claw of one and the right claw of the other clamped on its far edges. Only these two carried anything; the others followed them at regular intervals or marched ahead of them. Harry swam to the front of the column where it was nearing a savannah of eelgrass. Ten meters ahead of the main body was a cluster of five proceeding in a star configuration, and to each side of the star, ten or twelve feet out, was a single crab moving in unison with those that made up the star's points.

Harry motioned to Bruce to come toward him. They were above the foremost part of the column, the forward scouts in the eelgrass now. Bruce descended until he was a meter above the column. It stopped, the crab directly below him standing erect, their claws up. Bruce pushed at the water before him with his hands, and kicked. He began to rise.

Harry went out toward the point element and swam down, intending to grab one of them. They scattered and he selected the one closest to him and went after it into the eelgrass. It was surprisingly fast, faster than he was. He had chased crab before, for fun or food, but he had never come on one that could outrun him. He was astounded at its speed. He wanted to try another, but Bruce was in front of him, showing him with his hands that he had only six hundred pounds of air left. Harry looked at his gauge. The needle was a little below five hundred. Harry nodded his head and they swam together toward the beach.

"Have you ever seen anything like that?"

"No. Have you?"

Harry shook his head. "I've heard of lobster migrations, but I've never heard of crab doing it."

"That one little guy was fast. I saw you running after him."

"Yeah. I wonder if they're faster just after they molt and have new shells."

They were on the beach at Mukilteo, stripped down to their bathing suits, letting the sun warm them. The drying salt pulled the skin tight on Harry's back and face. It was a wonderful sunny day; when they went in the water, it was gray and drizzly. Harry felt very good. He felt a sense of completeness as he hardly ever did after a dive, and never in anything else he did. It was the combination of sun and warmth and the salt drying and the effort he had made in going after that crab.

"What do you think of that white thing those two crab were holding onto?"

"That thing like a shirt, or what was left of one? Yeah. I'm trying not to think about that," Bruce said.

"They eat us and we eat them."

"Stop."

"The things we've seen," Harry said. "Remember that half-blind lingcod at Edmonds?"

"Yeah. Yeah."

"And that skate as big as a barn door?"

"You told me about it. They don't get as big as barn doors, though."

"Little barns. For Shetland ponies."

Bruce gave out a laugh that ended in a snort.

"I once saw two eels mating," Harry said. "They were pure white. I mean whiter than anything I'd ever seen, or seen since. At first I didn't know what I was looking at. All I saw was this white ball about the size of a soccer ball, about twenty feet down. This was in Samoa at a break in the reef by Faga'alu."

"Say that again."

"Faga'alu. It's the name of a village. I lived there for a while after I left the army. After a lot of things. I was snorkeling and I saw this white ball on the sand right below me. And then it split apart and it was two snow-white eels, whiter even than snow. And they faced each other and then came together again, almost in a fury, it happened so fast and so violently. Maybe it was real fury, whatever that might be to eels. In a second they were so wrapped around each other you could not see where one left off and the other began. I remember thinking, 'Maybe that's why they call it balling.' But how many people have seen eels balling? I had a friend there, Chuck Brugman, who had spent most of his life diving in the Pacific, and I asked him if he'd ever heard of white eels, but he hadn't."

"Maybe they were congers."

"Congers are gray."

"Albino congers?" He was being impish.

"Who knows. Though this was in daylight and the sun was directly on them."

"Yeah, you'd think they'd stay indoors during the day and watch TV. Or sleep. They could have been vampire albino congers."

Harry stared at him. Bruce laughed but Harry continued to stare.

"Don't say it," Bruce said. "You're thinking, 'Speaking of balling, what's Janice been up to?' But I don't want to hear it."

Harry laughed. He couldn't help it. "Goddamn! We've known each other too long."

Bruce laughed again, not the little-boy laugh or the snorting laugh or any other that bespoke something else, but one that was straightforward and unaffected, and then he said, "I didn't know you lived in Samoa. My grandfather was there during the war. World War Two."

"I had an odd experience in Samoa once. I was diving with Chuck on the reef at Faganeanea—"

"Jeez. These names. Call it something else. Call it Albert."

"You call it Albert." Harry was annoyed. He wanted to tell this story and he wanted to tell it without bowdlerizing it. "So I was out with Chuck and we left the boat and were following the anchor chain down, and Chuck peeled off at about forty feet—he had said he was going to look for a particular shell he had spotted there on another dive—but I decided to go a little farther and then, without even thinking about it, I was on the bottom at a hundred and thirty-five feet."

"Were you using nitrogen?"

"They don't have that there. Just compressed air."

"Jesus, Harry."

"I know. But that's what I did. I had expected to feel the effects of narcosis—you know, nausea, loss of peripheral vision—"

"I don't get nauseated."

"Okay, but I do. But this time I didn't. So I'm on the bottom and I look around and in the distance is a blue light, like a wall coming up off the floor of the ocean, like the aurora borealis but a bright, metallic blue, and I start swimming toward it—"

"Jesus."

"I know. And I swim for a while but I'm not getting any closer, and then it occurs to me: I'm alone at a hundred and thirty-five feet and I'm swimming toward something that may not exist and I'm gobbling air like there will always be more than I need, and I check my air gauge and there's enough left so that, if I suck every last ounce out of the tank, I can get back to the surface even with decompression. And so I go back to the anchor chain and start climbing back up. I pass Chuck on the way—he's still messing around on the reef, near the surface now—and I wave to him but I don't stop. It's really hard to get air now. It's like I'm looking for it, but it's at a premium and it's hiding—well, you know how it feels to run out of air. And I pop the surface and clamber up on the boat and take my gear off and wait to see if I get a headache. Sometimes, if I haven't decompressed long enough, I get a headache, but this time I don't. And then Chuck is on the surface and he hands me his fins and he gets himself up onto the boat and he asks me if I saw that big blacktip on the reef, he was trying to point it out to me when I was on my way up, but either I didn't see him sign or I didn't understand what he was saying. Which was probably to my benefit because I couldn't have stopped, shark or no shark."

"That's why you should always leave some air in your tank. You don't know what's going to happen on your way in. Or up."

"I know. I'm real careful now. Honest. I do wonder about that blue light though, what it was, or was it only in my head. And was there something on the other side of it, or is that how everything ends."

"Jeez, Harry, cut it out. You're making me nervous. How come you didn't have a premonition about all of this before the dive? Or did you?"

"No."

"Well, where are they when you really need one?"

"I sometimes ask myself that."

"Did you tell Chuck about the blue light?"

"No. I didn't want him to think I was a fool."

"I don't know who's the fool, to separate like that. Both of you were diving alone."

"Well, I used to think that as far as Chuck was concerned, if you were in the ocean at the same time he was, you were buddies."

"Is that when you started to like diving solo?"

"I don't know. I never thought about it. I don't know."

At fifteen feet, he saw a brown rockfish nestled against a black rock. Some of its color was so light as to appear yellow. It was odd that it was so still. As he swam nearer, it barely moved, perhaps an inch or two, and then it settled back against the rock. Had the rock not been there, the fish would have gone completely onto its side. Its mouth opened and closed as if it were gasping for breath, though of course it was not. But its gills were working, so he knew it was alive, if in trouble.

He swam farther out. The water was unusually clear. He had never seen such luxuriant floral growth in the Sound. A plant whose name he could never remember but which reminded him of a juniper tree extended twenty feet toward the surface. He saw flounder and some blue perch and a couple of neon green gunnels. There were plenty of jellyfish feeding on those white anemones with the fluffy crowns. He almost swam into one with five-foot-long tentacles. It was the largest he'd seen outside of the tropics or California. He could see bits of white fluff through its skin.

On the way back to the beach, he found the rockfish in the same place he had seen it earlier. He touched its head with his finger, but it didn't move. Neither its mouth nor its gills moved. A slight tidal surge raised him off the bottom and he took advantage of it to coast in to shore.

All morning his shirt hung wrong on him, the neck sliding to one side, sliding again after he adjusted it. And all morning his tee shirt under it lay like needles on his skin, his body vaguely in pain. It was as though walking, sitting, standing, he were askew, as though he were somehow out of alignment. Getting into his wet suit, his muscles ached with an intensity beyond aching, and the skin on his arms and torso burned as though aflame, though only in patches. Yet he did not think to stop. Rather, it was as if he were bound to do what he would, regardless of his fear.

They were diving off Columbia Beach. The water was calm, there was no wind. The bottom was sand and silt held by eelgrass. They were near the ferry dock; it would be difficult to get confused about direction even if you didn't have a compass.

They were in only twelve feet of water when he lost Bruce. Bruce was on his right and then he wasn't. He wasn't anywhere. Harry came to the surface and waited. Then he snorkeled back to the beach. A boy ten or eleven was walking toward him on the path from the restaurant parking lot above the rocks overlooking the beach. A man was behind the boy about forty feet. Harry asked the boy if he'd seen another diver within the last few minutes. The boy shook his head. Harry took his weight belt off, then his tank and buoyancy compensator. The boy and the man were watching the water that was so motionless now it might have been freighted with oil. The sun's glare off the surface forced Harry to turn his eyes away. He had the sensation that he had stepped outside of time and he looked at his watch to see how much time had passed since they entered the water. He asked the man to call the Coast Guard and the Sheriff's Office. He would wait where he was in case Bruce turned up.

The man had just started up the hill when Bruce stood up out of the water. He had a rockfish thrashing on the shaft of his spear and he was carrying his fins. His lips moved and then he let go of the spear and fell into the water.

"I can't breathe. I don't know what's wrong."

Harry got Bruce's weights and tank and b.c. off and, with the help of the man, got him to the beach and laid him on his back on the sand.

"I can't breathe."

He hardly had the words out when his irises rolled up inside his head. Harry performed CPR, alone at first, then with another man who suddenly appeared until the ambulance arrived and the medical technicians took over. When Harry compressed his chest, Bruce's eyes rolled forward, then rolled back when Harry stopped to blow into his mouth. But after a few minutes they froze halfway up under the lids. By the time the ambulance got there, his lips were turning blue.

The mound of earth beside the grave was dry. It must have been excavated yesterday, maybe even the day before, Harry thought. Then he thought, Of course it was dug yesterday. Who's going to come out here at dawn to dig a grave?

He had not seen Janice in almost two years. He had forgotten how compact she was, how boyish her face. He had always expected to see a smudge of dirt on her cheek or nose. He saw Bruce's father whom he had met once, but did not say anything to him. Bruce's father saw him too, but also chose not to speak.

Walking to his car after the service, he heard a woman's heels and turned and saw Janice walking rapidly in his direction.

"Harry."

The embrace felt good. Her fragrance was nice.

"I hoped I would see you."

"It's good to see you," he said.

"His family ignored me. Even Jennifer. It was as if we had never met."

"They always were sort of self-contained. They ignored me too."

"It was his heart, wasn't it? Somebody said it was."

"That's what it looked like. I don't know if they did an autopsy."

"His uncle also died of a heart attack when he was really young. His father must be wondering about the genes he passed on."

"Does his father think like that?"

"I don't know. I didn't know him very well. You were there, weren't you? With Bruce? When he died?"

"Yes."

"I'm sorry."

Harry nodded his head.

"He was a good friend to me," Janice said. "He was my good friend." Harry thought she would cry after she said it the second time, but all there was was a catch in her voice which she quickly swallowed. "Even after all this time. I could tell him anything, because he knew me so well."

She was looking at the pavement. She was smiling. She looked up at him.

"You haven't changed, Harry. I was hoping you hadn't. It's nice when something remains the same."

They were standing at his car. The morning chill had faded and the sun was warm on his face.

"What about you? How have you been?" he asked.

"I've been well. I'm in the doctoral program now."

"Arizona?"

"Yes. Archeology. I actually like it. I was surprised that I took to it so well. I was afraid I would hate it."

Was her front tooth chipped? No, that was his imagination.

"Well," he said.

"I have to go. I have to catch a plane at one. I have to be at a conference in the morning and I still need to rehearse my presentation. It's okay, I rented a car. Did I tell you I met someone? I'll call you and tell you about him."

One of the kids told Harry that Brien had broken his window. Mike went to check on him while Harry opened the blood-spill kit, put on gloves, gown, boots, started for Brien's room. Halfway there, Mike met him, said blood was everywhere. Harry stopped his progress, asked Mike to fasten the gown's ties behind him, it was flapping between his legs. (Time, time—everything takes forever. But this was the age of AIDS, and the boy had been a prostitute.)

Brien was sitting on his bed, his back against the far wall. His left arm was extended—there were fresh cuts but they had stopped bleeding. His right hand was pressed against the side of his neck. Harry thought he may have cut his neck or stabbed himself and was trying now to stanch the flow of blood. There was blood on his right hand but it had dried—it must have come from his punching the window. The right side of his head and torso were in shadow. Maybe two seconds had passed since Harry opened the door to his room. Harry was standing at its threshold. He asked Brien what was wrong, then stepped into the room.

Brien had a large shard of glass in his right hand and was holding it against his neck. When Harry saw it he drew back. He said, "Come on, Brien. Give it to me." Brien was terribly frightened. He was nearly unconscious with fright. Suns burned dimly in his pale eyes. Harry felt his balance shift. In Brien's gray eyes Harry saw worlds not his own.

Brien made a quick downward motion with his hand and Harry heard something tear. Before he could move, Brien replaced the glass against his neck. Harry saw no fresh blood. Then—he didn't know why; he could think of nothing else to do—he grasped Brien's other hand and pressed it gently. As though he had been waiting for this specific signal, Brien threw the glass down on his bed and Mike came in and picked it up. Harry looked at Brien's neck where he had stroked the glass across it. It was raw but was not bleeding.

For a moment after Mike took Brien out of his room Harry sat on his bed, pulling himself out of his eyes, away from the planets orbiting his fear. For a moment, two...

Until he reached sixty feet he had not known what he intended, but at sixty feet he decided to continue down into the pit where, decades earlier, they had dredged the bottom to allow the oil tankers in. Ninety feet and down. In a moment he would feel a rush of heat roll up his body, beginning at his feet and washing like a wave to his head, always, for him, the first indication of nitrogen narcosis. Then he would lose his peripheral vision and get the taste of bile in his mouth. At a hundred and twenty feet his skin would get numb, as though it were covered with an additional layer immune to tactile sensation, and his mind would split from itself. Part of it would observe everything around him and another part would tell him that the first part was lying and that he should not believe what it saw and heard. Once, only once, did a third part reveal itself, and it told him that he should not believe either the first part of his mind or the second part, neither what he saw and heard nor the doubting of them.

But he did not experience either the doubt or the doubt of both doubt and certainty this time. At a hundred and thirty-five feet he leveled off and aimed for a wall of sapphire light in the distance. His body was very warm and he was sweating inside his wet suit. He swam for several minutes but he seemed to get no closer and he began to question how this shimmering blue glow could exist in a place without sun, where light graduated in its quality only between dusk and deep night. He began to wonder if he had made a mistake by going so far and he began to ascend.

All Air is Finite

I knew a boy who killed a man by dropping a rock off a bridge through the windshield of his passing car. After two years the boy had convinced himself that the rock had dropped itself.

The hardest story I ever heard, though one that ever repeats itself, concerns a boy who, diving a shipwreck at ninety feet with his father, witnesses his father's getting tangled in a murk of cables and cannot extricate him. Ultimately his father sends him to the surface—all air is finite, a son's no less than a father's—to locate help, but of course the only help he can find is the help that will bring up the body.

This is as far as the story goes.

But there are questions. What would the boy have told himself? Certainly he would recognize eventually that his father, grasping the fact of his imminent death, had saved his son by sending him off in search of illusory help. And inevitably the boy would have asked himself what more he could have done.

But would he have asked himself when exactly did he know his father would die? Was it when he left him? Was it during his ascent? Or was it only on that sun-bright surface, that more common world of foot motility and unencumbered speech, that he understood at last that all air is finite? Would the boy, after two years or three of grief, have persuaded himself to despise his father for dying as he committed his son to live?

What did the boy do with his life? Did he mutilate it with

drugs? Did he end it with a gun? Did he hide in a monastery or a university? Did he marry, beat his wife, murder his children?

The boy who dropped the rock that dropped itself went to prison, served his time, got out. I lost track of him, though I heard stories, unverified.

The second boy got life.

Jerome Gold is the author of fourteen books, including *The Moral Life of Soldiers*, *Sergeant Dickinson*, and *Paranoia & Heartbreak: Fifteen Years in a Juvenile Facility*, a memoir of the years he spent as a rehabilitation counselor in a prison for children. He has lived in or near Seattle for more than half his life.